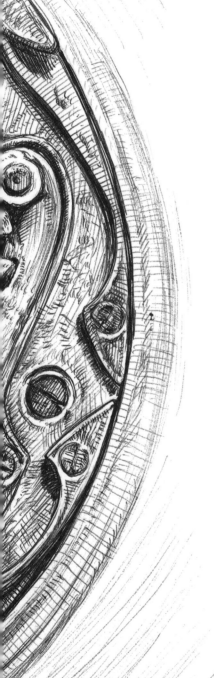

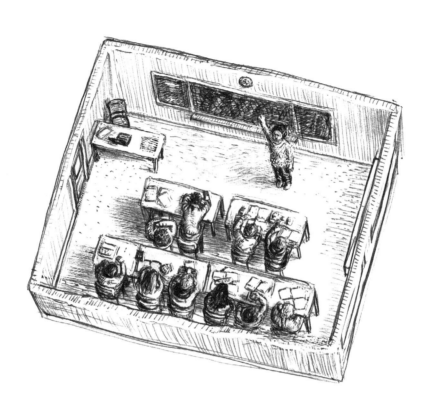

ONE MINUTE'S SILENCE

written by
David Metzenthen

illustrated by
Michael Camilleri

ALLEN&UNWIN
SYDNEY·MELBOURNE·AUCKLAND·LONDON

In one minute's silence....

…you can imagine the grinding in your guts as the ironbark bows of the Australian boats bumped the stony shore of Gallipoli on the twenty-fifth of April, 1915…

when twelve thousand wild colonial boys dashed across
the shivering Turkish sand in the pale light of a dairy
farmer's dawn lashed with flying lead.

But can you imagine, in one minute's silence, lines of young Turkish soldiers from distant villages, hearts hammering, standing shoulder-to-shoulder in trenches cut like wounds…

firing on the strangers wading through the shallows,
intent on streaming into the homeland of the
Turkish people.

In one minute's silence, you can imagine the boys from the back of beyond, and the blokes from the big smoke, mad-scrambling up the steepest of Turkish slopes…

making tracks and marking maps with skidding boots and bursts of blood as they blasted and bayoneted their way through the scrub.

But can you imagine, in one minute's silence,
how the Turks, fighting for their land and their lives,
felt when they saw the enemy battleships anchored in the bay,
slouch-hatted strangers swarming towards them with rifles...

and knew that this was going
to be a fight to the death.

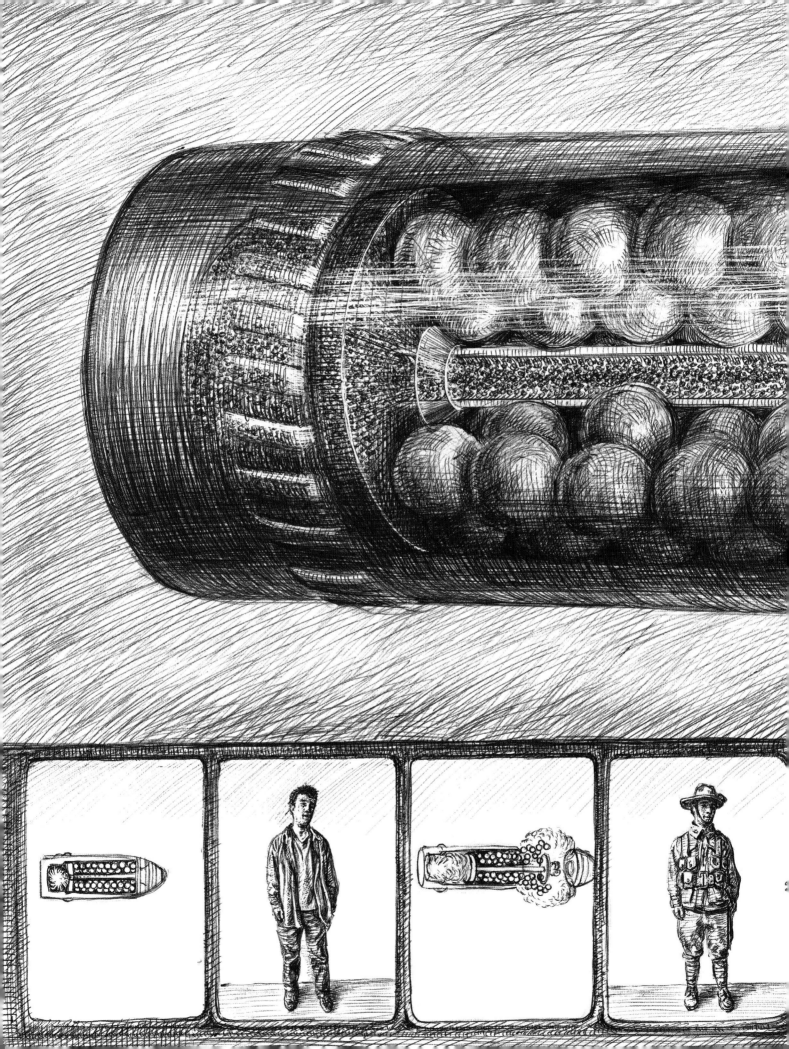

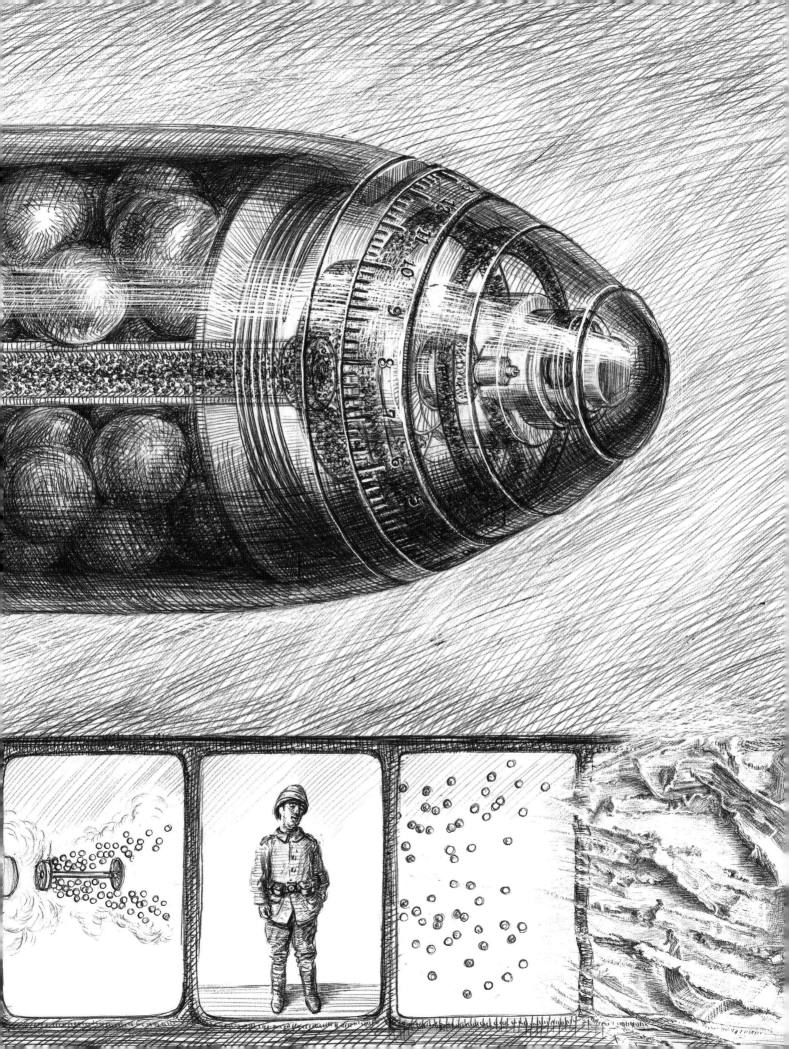

In one minute of silence, you can imagine the bare-knuckled bushmen of the Australian Lighthorse ten seconds away from running at the Turkish machine-guns, turning to each other to say, 'See ya later, mate…'

then going like mad until just about each and
every one was stopped dead in his tracks.

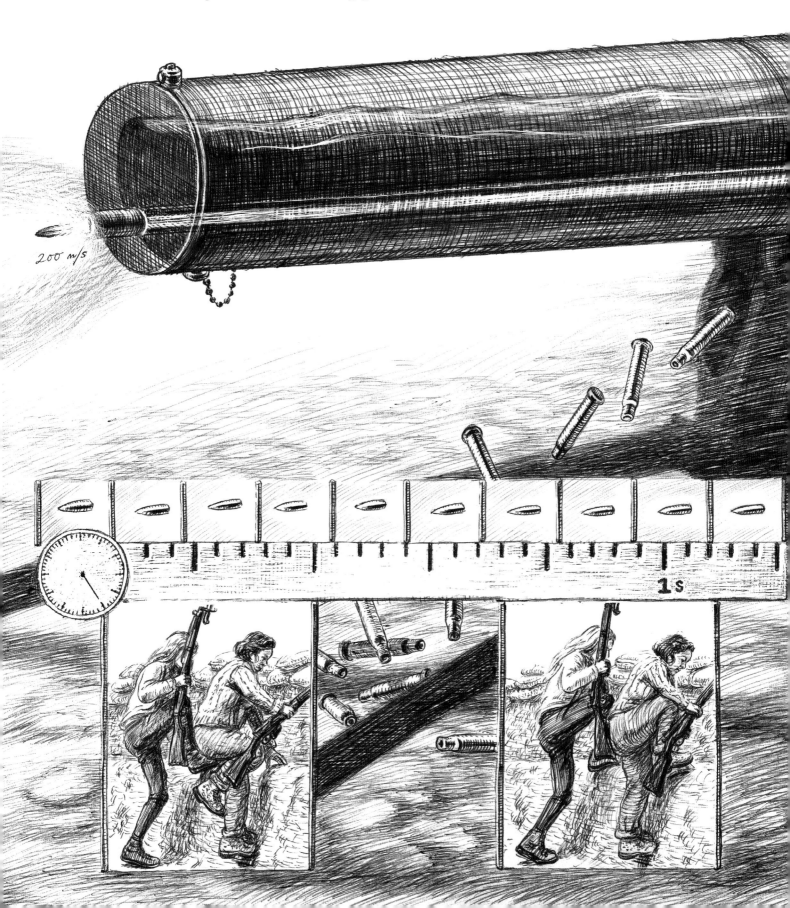

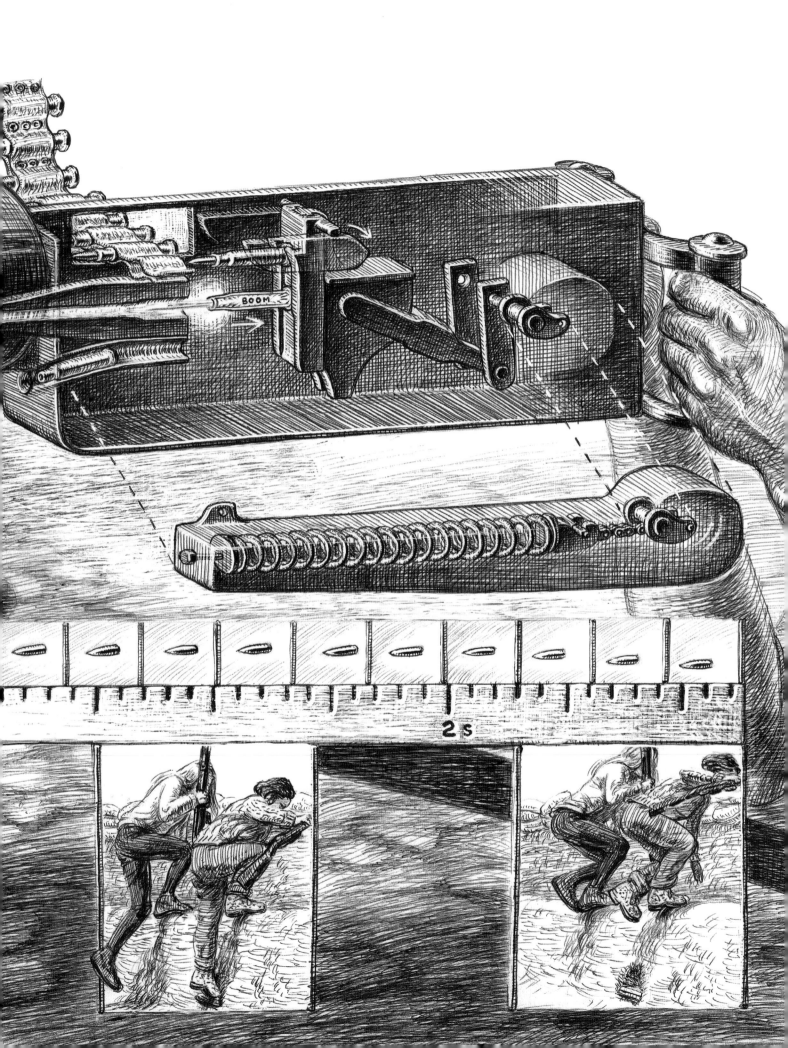

BOOM

2 s

But can you imagine, in one minute's silence, when it was the Turkish soldiers who charged again and again until the ground was strewn with thousands of dead and dying men...

and the cries of the wounded, in words
the Anzacs did not know but understood,
filled the sky and reached the sea.

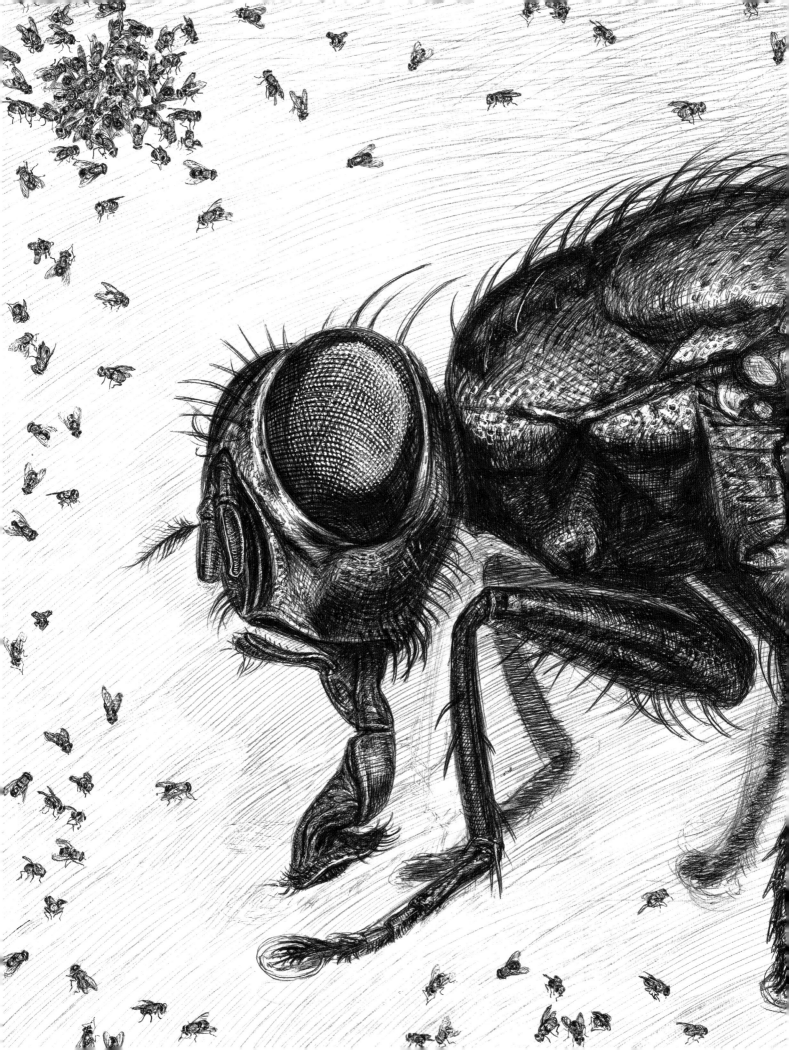

In one minute's silence, you can imagine the solitary
day when these men met without weapons, sharing
cigarettes and shovels as they buried their dead
in the cool Turkish earth…

and the sound of the wind and waves,
and quiet talking, replaced the crack,
boom, and blast of war.

But can you imagine the fierce Anzacs and
the fighting Turks quietly returning to their
trenches after this one day of truce...

then firing at each other that afternoon,
although they truly knew that the other
men were not so much different after all.

In one minute's silence, can you imagine what the Turkish fighters felt when they knew they could hold the high ground…

and the rain that lashed them felt like tears of joy.

And can you imagine, in one minute's silence, the moment when the bloodied Diggers finally reached the razored heights of Gallipoli where the Lone Pine grew…

to see that the
hazy Turkish horizon was as
impossible to reach as a castle in the clouds.

And you can imagine, in one
minute's silence, as the Turkish
fighters stood strong and straight
in their freezing trenches…

that the dream they dreamed,
of going home, circled like a
dove that might soon settle
in quietened hearts.

In one minute's silence, you can imagine the Anzacs strengthening their front lines as if to fight through every hour of every day of the bitter Turkish winter…

yet in secret they were preparing to leave the
cliffs and beaches of Gallipoli seven days
before Christmas in 1915.

But can you imagine, in one minute's silence, as the Turkish fighters looked down from the cliffs…

that the Anzacs were binding their boots in cloth, leaving presents and notes, and rifles rigged to fire, and about to make their way down to the sea and the waiting ships.

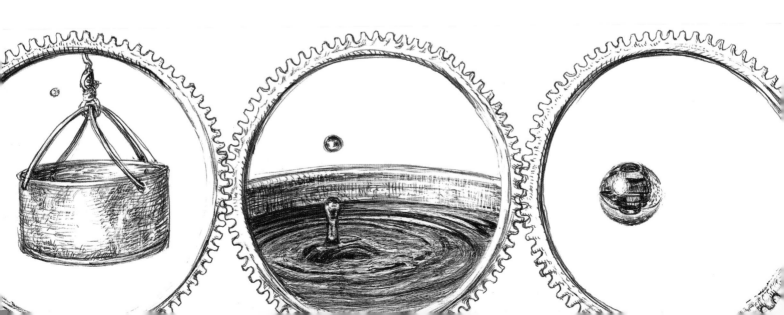

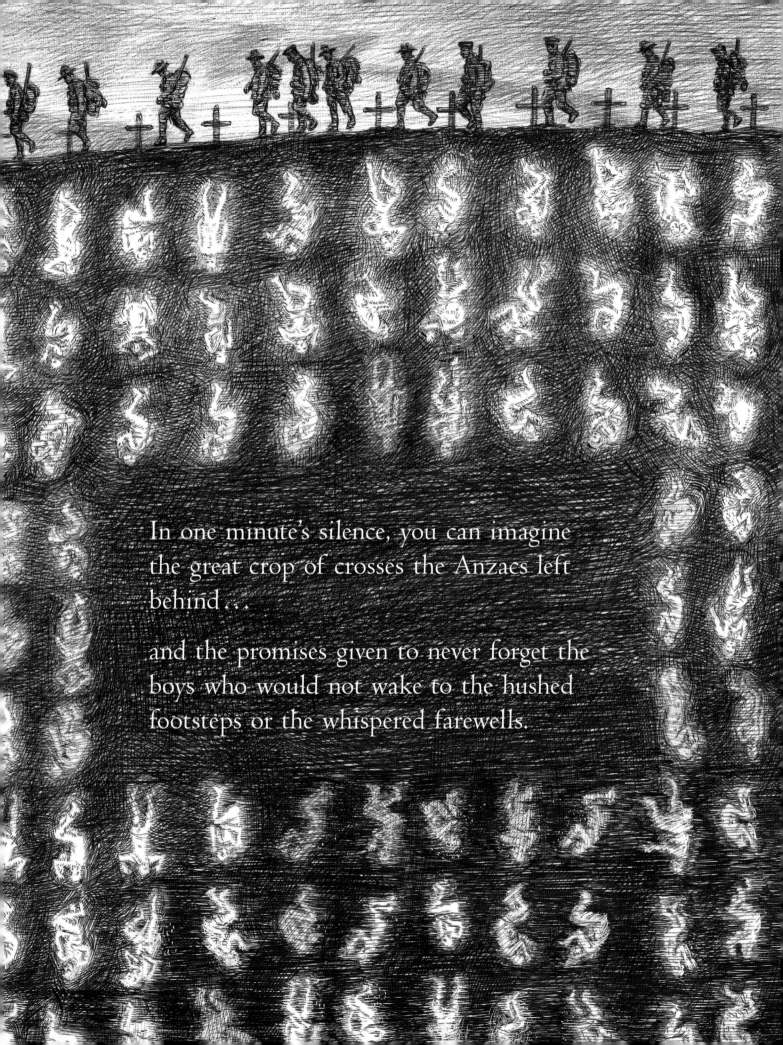

In one minute's silence, you can imagine
the great crop of crosses the Anzacs left
behind...

and the promises given to never forget the
boys who would not wake to the hushed
footsteps or the whispered farewells.

But can you imagine, in one minute's silence, when the Turkish soldiers rose that morning to discover there only remained…

the perfect lack of sound of a war that had ended.

THOSE HEROES THAT SHED THEIR BLOOD AND LOST
THEIR LIVES... YOU ARE NOW LYING IN THE SOIL OF
A FRIENDLY COUNTRY. THEREFORE REST IN PEACE.
THERE IS NO DIFFERENCE BETWEEN THE JOHNNIES
AND THE MEHMETS TO US WHERE THEY LIE SIDE
BY SIDE, HERE IN THIS COUNTRY OF OURS... YOU,
THE MOTHERS, WHO SENT THEIR SONS FROM FAR
AWAY COUNTRIES WIPE AWAY YOUR TEARS; YOUR
SONS ARE NOW LYING IN OUR BOSOM AND ARE
IN PEACE. AFTER HAVING LOST THEIR LIVES ON THIS
LAND THEY HAVE BECOME OUR SONS AS WELL.

ATATÜRK 1934

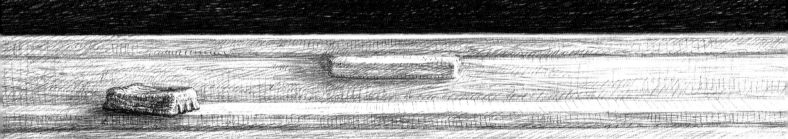

In memory of the Anzacs and the Turkish troops who fought with honour on the Gallipoli Peninsula (Galibolu),
25 April 1915 to 20 December 1915. – DM

Michael Camilleri would like to thank Sophia Mundi Steiner School and the Year 12 Class of 2013.

First published in 2014

Allen & Unwin
83 Alexander Street
Crows Nest NSW 2065 Australia
Phone: (61 2) 8425 0100
Email: info@allenandunwin.com   Web: www.allenandunwin.com

A Cataloguing-in-Publication entry is available from the National Library of Australia www.trove.nla.gov.au

ISBN 978 1 74331 624 5

Teachers' notes available from www.allenandunwin.com

Design by Sandra Nobes
Colour reproduction by Splitting Image, Clayton, Victoria
Printed in May 2014 at Hang Tai Printing (Guang Dong) Ltd., Xin Cheng Ind Est,
Xie Gang Town, Dong Guan, Guang Dong Province, China.

1 3 5 7 9 10 8 6 4 2

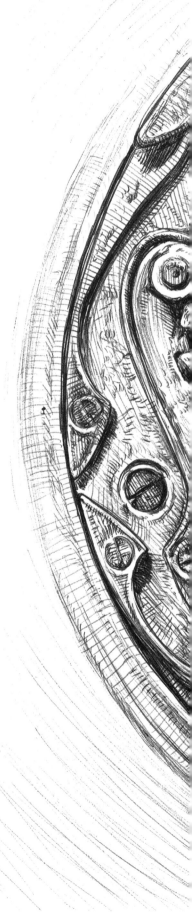